TINA
the tiniest girl

Also by Laurence Anholt and Tony Ross
Orchard Crunchies: One and Only Series
Ruby the Rudest Girl
Harold the Hairiest Man
Boris the Brainiest Baby
Polly the most Poetic Person
Bruno the Bravest Man
Ben the Bendiest Boy

By Laurence Anholt and Arthur Robins
Orchard Super Crunchies: Seriously Silly Stories Series
Cinderboy
Daft Jack and the Beanstack
Billy Beast
Rumply Crumply Stinky Pin
The Emperor's Underwear
The Rather Small Turnip
The Fried Piper of Hamstring
Little Red Riding Wolf
Snow White and the Seven Aliens

ORCHARD BOOKS
96 Leonard Street, London EC2A 4RH
Orchard Books Australia
14 Mars Road, Lane Cove, NSW 2066
First published in Great Britain in 1999
First paperback publication 2000
Text © Laurence Anholt 1999
Illustrations © Tony Ross 1999
The rights of Laurence Anholt to be identified as the
author and Tony Ross as the illustrator of this work
have been asserted by them in accordance with the
Copyright, Designs and Patents Act, 1988.
A CIP catalogue record for this book is available
from the British Library.
1 86039 980 0 (hardback)
1 86039 981 9 (paperback)
Printed in Great Britain

TINA
the tiniest girl

Laurence Anholt

Illustrated by Tony Ross

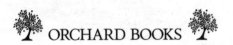 ORCHARD BOOKS

We are going to meet Tina.
We are going to meet the one
and only Tina, the tiniest girl
in the world.
But where is she?

I cannot see Tina anywhere.
Perhaps Tina has gone out today.

Wait. Wait there. I will go and get
my magnifying glass.

Now we can see her. Now we can see Tina, the teeniest, weeniest cutest girl who ever lived.

Tina is so tiny that she sleeps in a
pencil-case.

And has a bath in a teacup.

And goes for a ride on a roller skate.

Wherever she goes, people stop
and smile.

Tina is so tiny and so cute they all
want to give her a big cuddle.

Lots of people have small brothers and sisters at home, but NO ONE is quite as small and quite as sweet as Tina. That is why everybody loves her.

Tina's dad is not tiny. He is quite tall.

Tina's dad has a pet shop.
Sometimes Tina sits on the counter
or plays on a hamster wheel.

Everyone loves to come to the
pet shop.
They cuddle the kittens.

They hold the hamsters.

They pat the puppies.

Most of all they come to kiss
Tina, the tiniest girl in the world.

But sometimes Tina gets fed up
with being small. Especially when
she gets knocked over by a big
bouncy rabbit or when she falls
into a goldfish bowl.

Then Tina says,

Tina's dad knows everything about looking after pets. If anyone has a problem with their pet, they ask Tina's dad.

Tina's dad has Tortoise Tablets
for tortoises who won't wake up.

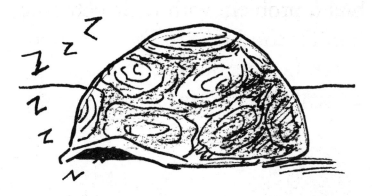

And Parrot Pills for parrots who
won't talk.

One day a lady comes in to the
shop. She has a small dog that
will not grow.
Tina's dad looks at the little dog.
Then he gets out a bottle of
Doggy Grow Drops.

"You must be careful," says Tina's dad. "These Doggy Grow Drops are VERY strong! If you give your dog ONE drop too many, he will grow as big as a DONKEY! If you give your dog TWO drops too many, he will grow as big as a DINOSAUR!"

The lady goes home to try the
Doggy Grow Drops.
Tina has been listening. She has
heard all about the VERY
STRONG Doggy Grow Drops.

If I have some of
those Doggy Grow Drops,
I will grow big too.

Her dad is busy with a hamster
who has a headache. Tina climbs
onto a high shelf and takes a
bottle of Doggy Grow Drops.

Tina opens the bottle. She needs something to try the Doggy Grow Drops on. She sees a baby woodlouse on the floor. Tina gives ONE tiny drop to the baby woodlouse.

The woodlouse begins to grow...

Up...

and up...

and UP.

Until it grows as big as a
guinea pig.

"Mmm, these Doggy Grow Drops
are quite strong," says Tina.
She gives TWO of the Doggy
Grow Drops to a hamster.
The hamster begins to grow...

Up...

and up...

and UP.

Until it grows as big as a pony.

"These Doggy Grow Drops are VERY strong," says Tina, and she finishes the WHOLE BOTTLE! Tina begins to grow...

Up...

and up...

and UP!

We are going to meet Tina.
We are going to meet Tina again.
But where is she?

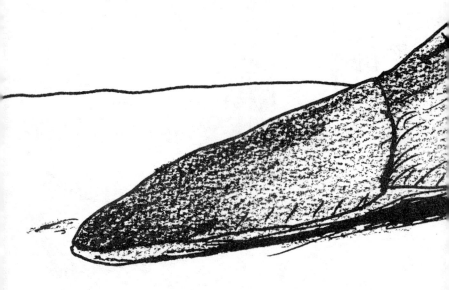

I cannot see Tina anywhere.
Perhaps Tina has gone out today.

Wait. Wait there. I will go and get my helicopter.

Now we can see her. Now we can
see Tina, the BIGGEST, most
ENORMOUS girl who ever lived.

Tina is bigger than a cow. Tina is bigger than a camel. Tina is bigger than KING KONG!

Where are you going? Why is
everybody running away? Don't
you want to kiss Tina any more?

Tina's dad comes running. He has a big box. It is a box of VERY strong Pink Shrink Poodle Powder. He gives Tina one spoonful.

Tina begins to shrink...

Down...

and down...

and down.

Now here is Tina next to the
counter in the pet shop.

Tina is not too big. Tina is not
too small.
She is exactly the right size.
And everybody loves her.